The Rugrats' Easter Surprise

KLaSKY
CSUPO INC.

Based on the TV series *Rugrats*® created by Arlene Klasky, Gabor Csupo, and
Paul Germain as seen on Nickelodeon®

SIMON SPOTLIGHT
An imprint of Simon & Schuster Children's Publishing Division
1230 Avenue of the Americas
New York, New York 10020

Manufactured in the United States of America

First Edition
2 4 6 8 10 9 7 5 3 1

ISBN 0-689-84742-4

The Rugrats' Easter Surprise

Adapted by Sarah Willson
from the screenplay by Scott Gray
Illustrated by Robert Roper

Simon Spotlight/Nickelodeon

New York   London   Toronto   Sydney   Singapore

One sunny spring day the babies were playing in the Pickleses' backyard.

"Wow! Everything's so purple!" said Tommy. "Um . . . I mean blue. I get my colors mixed up sometimes."

"Look at all the prettyful flowers!" said Lil.

Suddenly Tommy's dog, Spike, ran up and playfully knocked him to the grass.

Tommy giggled. "My favoritest part of spring is that I get to play outside with my bestest doggy friend!"

"Thanks for helping us with our Easter brunch tomorrow," said Chas.
"We've been so busy planning it, we haven't even had time to give Fifi her spring haircut!" said Kira, looking down at Fifi's fluffy fur coat. "Wait until you see our backyard. The bushes are sculpted to look like little bunnies and chicks!"

"That's right, we're going all-out!" said Chas. "Springtime is the season for love, so this is our way of celebrating ours." He and Kira looked adoringly at each other.

"It's important to keep romance alive, don't you think, Stu?" asked Didi. But Stu didn't seem to hear her.

Outside, Spike was playing fetch with Tommy. Suddenly Spike dropped his stick and ran off.

"Spike, wait!" called Tommy. "Come back! We're not done playin'!"

But Spike paid no attention.

"I wonder why Spike runned off with Fifi so fast," said Tommy.

Angelica snorted. "Don't you babies know nothin'?" she said. "It's obvious what's wrong with Spike. He's in love!"

"Well, that eggsplains it then," said Tommy. "Uh . . . what's 'in love'?"

"Oh, brother," said Angelica. "I guess it's up to me to tell you about the birds and the fleas. See, Spike falled in love with Fifi, and now he's forgotted all about you!"

"Hey, Spike!" Tommy called to his dog. "It's me, Tommy! Your bestest baby friend!"
Spike turned and licked Fifi's ear.

"It looks like he doesn't 'member you," said Kimi gently.

"When my daddy forgets stuff, he ties stringies to his finger so he'll 'member," said Lil.

"Good idea, Lil!" said Tommy. "Let's go find some string!"

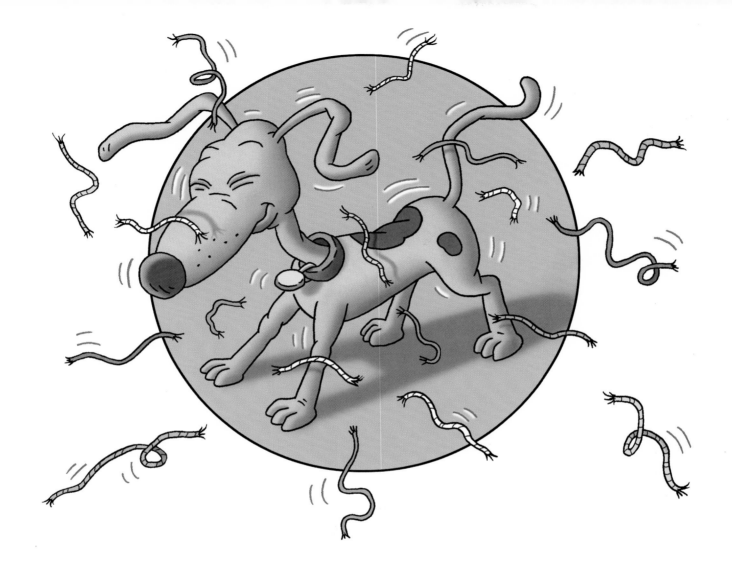

The babies found some strings and then draped them all over Spike.

"C'mon, Spike! 'Member me!" said Tommy. But the strings didn't seem to help.

"I guess we shoulda tied the strings," he said as Spike shook them off.

"We don't know how to tie yet," Phil reminded him.

"Give it up, Tommy!" said Angelica. "Spike's never gonna remember you. He's in love."

"My daddy and new mommy love each other," said Chuckie, "but they still 'member me and Kimi."

"That's 'cause they're married!" said Angelica. "Once ya get married, you stop being all lovey-dovey 'cause you're busy puttin' buns in the oven and stuff."

"Well, Spike and Fifi are in the lovey-dovey part right now," said Chuckie, "so next they gotta get married. Then Spike will 'member you, Tommy!"

"Oooh, a wedding," said Angelica dreamily. "I'm in charge!"

Meanwhile, Didi was doing some spring cleaning. "I'm throwing away some of your broken inventions," she said to Stu, a bit huffily.

Stu bounded over to the trash can. "Not my sonic insect repeller, Deed!" he said. "It'll be perfect for the brunch tomorrow."

"Frankly, Stu," said Didi, "I think you should be spending more time with me and less time with your inventions. After all, spring is the season of love!"

"Exactly!" said Stu, taking her by the hand. "Come with me. I want to show you what I've been working on."

"Oh, Stu!" breathed Didi. "I love it!"

In the backyard the doggy wedding was about to begin.

"Throw the flowers!" Angelica hissed at Kimi. "Never work with babies and animals," she muttered to herself. Then she pointed at Tommy to begin.

"Dearly blubbered," he said, "we are here today to see the marrying of Spike and Fifi. Fifi, do you take Spike to be your awful wedded groom?"

Fifi scratched her ear.

"Uh . . . Spike, do you take Fifi to be your awful wedded bride?"

Spike barked at a squirrel.

"I now denounce you, uh . . . Mr. and Mrs. Spike and Fifi! You may kiss the bride!" said Tommy.

Spike licked Fifi's ear.

"Now Spike will 'member me!" said Tommy. "Here, Spike!"

But Spike paid no attention to Tommy.

"It didn't work!" said Tommy sadly.

"A-course not, Tommy!" said Angelica. "The wedding's not over. We need to throw rice and have the wedding recession. Then you gots to give them presents. That's the only good reason to get married!"

Kimi and Chuckie gave a rock to the dog couple. "I hope you guys don't gots one already," said Kimi.

Phil and Lil gave them bellybutton lint. "You can never gets enough lint," said Phil.

Tommy knelt down in front of Spike. "Here's your present. It's a picture of you and me. 'Member what good friends we were? You gots to 'member me, Spike, you just gots to, 'cause . . . I miss you."

Spike sniffed the frame, then turned back to Fifi.

"Chuckie, Kimi, Fifi!" Chas called. "Time to go home!"
Spike trotted after Fifi.
"Spike wants to go too!" said Kira.
"Well, it's fine with me if they want to have a play date," Didi
said, smiling. "I think Spike has a crush on Fifi."

A tear trickled down Tommy's cheek. "Spike just runned away with his new bride!" he sobbed. "He didn't even bark good-bye!"

"You'll see him at the bunch tomorrow, Tommy," soothed Lil.

"So what?" said Tommy. "My bestest doggy friend has forgotted all about me!"

That night, Tommy couldn't sleep. "I miss Spike," he cried to himself. "But I guess he's happy with Fifi now. So, if my friend's happy, I guess I gots to be too. Happy. Happy. Happy."

The next morning, everyone arrived at the Finsters' house. "Happy Easter, Charles!" said Didi. Stu hopped through the door, but he stopped short when he saw Chas, Howard, and Drew. "You could have at least called me," Stu said.

"It's almost time for the egg hunt!" said Chas.

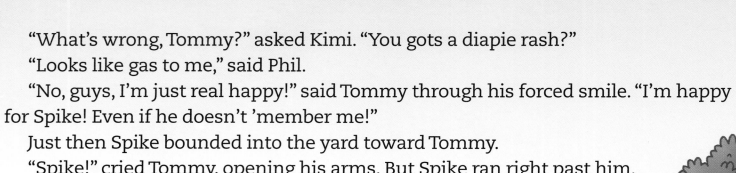

"What's wrong, Tommy?" asked Kimi. "You gots a diapie rash?"

"Looks like gas to me," said Phil.

"No, guys, I'm just real happy!" said Tommy through his forced smile. "I'm happy for Spike! Even if he doesn't 'member me!"

Just then Spike bounded into the yard toward Tommy.

"Spike!" cried Tommy, opening his arms. But Spike ran right past him.

"Time for the egg hunt!" called Chas.

A bee buzzed by. And then another. "I'll take care of those pesky bees!" said Stu, hurrying over to his sonic insect repeller.

As the babies went off to hunt for eggs, bees swarmed the backyard.

"I just remembered why I put my sonic insect repeller in the closet!" cried Stu. "It *attracts* insects!"

"There's an egg," said Tommy, dully.

"There's another one," said Kimi. "This game's kinda boring."

"Wanna go eat mud?" suggested Phil.

"Wait, you guys," said Tommy. "I'm not really happy. I was just pretendin'. I miss Spike. I'm real, real sad. . . ."

Suddenly he felt a tugging on his shirt.

"Look, Tommy, he 'members you!" cried Chuckie.
"Oh, Spike, I've missed you!" said Tommy. "Hey, I think he wants us to follow him!"
Tommy and his friends hurried after Spike.

The babies gasped when they saw where Spike had gone.
"Fifi and Spike gots a visit from the storch!" said Lil.
"They gots a visit from a lotta storches!" said Phil.
"So the onliest reason that Spike forgotted me was 'cause he knew he was gonna be a daddy doggy!" said Tommy happily.
"Easter babies!" said Kimi. "Aren't they cute?"
Tommy moved closer to Spike and whispered, "You're gonna like havin' babies around."